LOOSIE B. GOOSIE

Marilyn Webb Neagley

Illustrations by
Abby Stoner

Published by

WIND
RIDGE
BOOKS
of vermont

LOOSIE B. GOOSIE

Marilyn Webb Neagley

Illustrations by

Abby Stoner

Published by Wind Ridge Books of Vermont
P.O. Box 636
Shelburne, Vermont 05482

ISBN: 978-1-935922-16-2
Library of Congress Control Number: 2013938017

For my children and grandchildren. For all children.

This tale of kindness is based on a true story
that took place on Shelburne Farms
in Shelburne, Vermont.

One late summer day, on a farm by a shimmering lake, a white goose appeared out of nowhere. The poor goose had a badly broken wing. It could waddle but was unable to fly or swim. The goose was stranded.

A kind man and woman lived nearby in a brick house.

Each day they brought grain and water. They named the goose Loosie B. Goosie.

A second surprise arrived a few days later. Another goose appeared!
This goose had gray feathers, so the man and woman named it Gray.

Loosie B. Goosie was very excited to have this new friend.

The two geese spent their days eating and chattering together in a happy way.
"Honk, honk! What a good day this is!"

"Honk, honk! So glad to have you with me, my friend."

As summer turned to fall, everyone who lived on the farm wondered
what would happen to the geese when winter arrived

and the days grew dangerously cold.

One day a glorious gaggle of geese flew across the sky and
called out to Loosie and Gray,

"Come with us. Hurry! Winter is coming. It's time to fly south where it's sunny and warm."

At first, Gray refused to go with the other geese. "No, I want to stay here, with you."
Loosie insisted, "I can't fly with my broken wing, but you can.
I want you to be safe from the cold. Please go."

Even though it was very difficult to do, Gray agreed to join the other geese.
Loosie and Gray said goodbye to each other.

Gray and the other geese spent that evening in a farmer's field only a mile away.
They filled up on corn and prepared for their long trip south

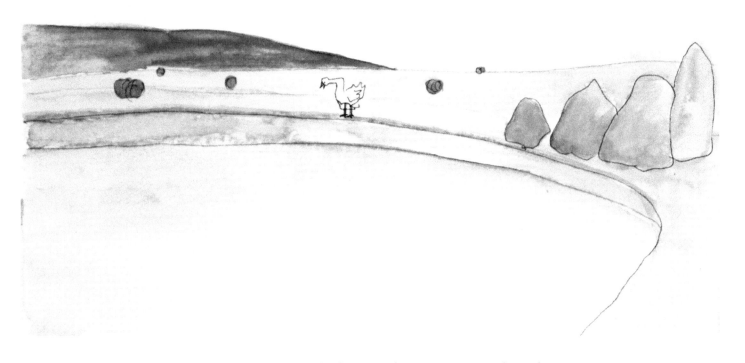

while Loosie stood alone, shivering on the shore.

That night, under a full moon, the two friends sadly called back and forth to each other, "Hoooonk, hoooonk, hoooonk."

The kind man and woman who had fed them could hear their mournful good-bye sounds and they too began to cry.

Soon the days grew chilly. The man and woman made a little house for Loosie. Loosie was frightened and didn't want to go in the house.

"Hisssss, hisssss! Leave me alone!" Loosie said. The kind man and woman worried that Loosie would not be able to survive the bitter cold of winter.

Suddenly they had an idea! Could Loosie live with someone who takes care of geese? The woman called a farmer named Clyde, who lived across the lake.

Clyde raised geese in a pleasant barn next to his home. He liked geese and knew how to speak their language.

Clyde crossed the lake on a ferryboat and drove to the farm, straight to Loosie.
He got out of his truck and held the door open. "C'mon, Loosie, hop in," he said.

22

Loosie instantly trusted Clyde and got right into the truck. They rode away together to the ferryboat and across the lake.

When they arrived, Loosie was overjoyed! The barn was full of cheerful geese and golden straw. It was almost perfect, but one thing was missing ... Loosie B. Goosie looked around to see if maybe, just maybe, Gray had found this friendly place.

OH! Do you see what Loosie saw!? Now it was the perfect home.

CPSIA information can be obtained at www.ICGtesting.com
Printed in the USA
LVOW021852050713

341617LV00012B/22/P